DISCARD

Callie Ann
⇥ and ⇤
Mistah Bear

retold by

Robert D. San Souci

pictures by Don Daily

Dial Books for Young Readers
New York

Published by Dial Books for Young Readers
A division of Penguin Putnam Inc.
345 Hudson Street • New York, New York 10014

Text copyright © 2000 by Robert D. San Souci
Pictures copyright © 2000 by Don Daily
Designed by Debora Smith and Atha Tehon
Printed in Hong Kong on acid-free paper
1 3 5 7 9 10 8 6 4 2

Library of Congress Cataloging in Publication Data
San Souci, Robert D.
Callie Ann and Mistah Bear/
retold by Robert D. San Souci; pictures by Don Daily.
p.   cm.
Summary: A bear disguised as a fine, handsome man comes courting
Callie Ann's mother and Callie Ann must outwit the bear
to prevent her mother from marrying it.
ISBN 0-8037-1766-0
[1. Afro-Americans—Folklore. 2. Folklore—United States.]
I. Daily, Don, ill. II. Title. PZ8.1.S227Cal 2000
398.2'089'96073—dc20   [E]   94-33171   CIP   AC

The art was painted in gouache on Strathmore Bristol plate.

For Dr. Louise Scott, in admiration,
appreciation, and deepest friendship
R.D.S.S.

For Charles Santore—
thanks for opening the door
D.D.

Callie Ann lived in the old times, when animals could talk. Her papa had died, so Callie Ann and her ma worked hard to make a go of their small farm. Many men courted the pretty widow. She refused them all.

Callie Ann wished her ma would marry Mose, who ploughed the fields. But her mamma just said, "He's a good man, but he's common as a shoe. I plan t' marry a quality gennelman."

"Yes'm," her daughter said. Still, Callie Ann thought good-natured, hardworking Mose would make a fine stepdaddy.

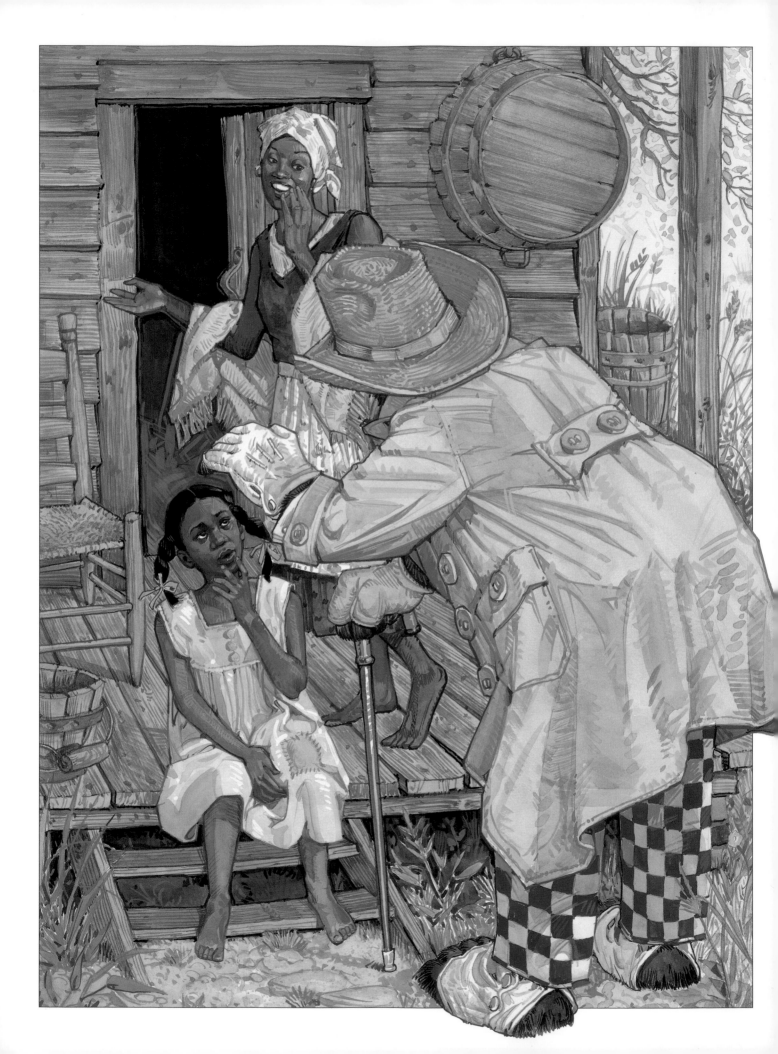

One day a stranger strolled up from the piney woods. He wore a fancy coat, white spats, and a broad hat pulled down low.

"I come t' pay respects, ma'am," he said with a bow. He patted Callie Ann's head with a hand big as a shovel and said, "Pretty little girlee you got—near as pretty as her ma."

"Thank you kindly," said Callie Ann's mother, smiling. "Do come inter the kitchen and set a spell." She whispered to Callie Ann, "Now here's a quality gennelman—see how well he's dressed."

The girl tried to be polite, but she couldn't help staring. The big fellow's chair groaned as he gobbled down sugar cookies and spooned the sugar bowl empty to sweeten his lemonade. And he always kept his hat brim between his face and the mother and daughter.

"You surely got a sweet tooth!" Callie Ann's ma exclaimed. "The cookies are gone, but I could fix biscuits 'n' honey."

"I won't say no, ma'am," the man answered. Well, the biscuits, swimming in honey, disappeared as fast as the cookies. When the stranger opened wide to swallow the last biscuits, Callie Ann saw he had a mouthful of big, sharp, yellow teeth.

Then the girl spotted brown fur peeping through a hole in one white spat. But when she tugged on her mamma's sleeve to show her, the woman scolded, "Chile! You're jumpy as a worm in hot ashes. Get you outside and leave us be."

So Callie Ann went and played with the dogs who were chained behind the house. Near evening the stranger left, saying, "I'll come callin' tomorrow."

Callie Ann followed him into the woods. There he pulled off his coat and trousers, and Callie Ann was scared to see it was really Mistah Bear!

Frightened, Callie Ann ran home and said, "Mamma, that fellow is really Mistah Bear who's just comin' t' eat whatever we got that's sweet!"

"Hush, chile!" her mother said. "Tellin' lies 'bout a quality gennelman! One more word and I'll send you t' bed with no supper!"

Callie Ann stayed awake most of the night, studying what to do. In the morning she found Mistah Bear sitting in the kitchen. He was drinking iced tea sugared thick as syrup, and gobbling molasses cookies.

Callie Ann shouted, "No more tricks, you ole bear, you!" And she knocked his hat clean off his head.

With a roar, Mistah Bear burst out of his clothes. Callie Ann and her ma ran out the door, shouting for Mose. Quick as a wink, Mose unchained the snarling, snapping dogs.

Mistah Bear shook his paw at Callie Ann. "You ain't seen the last of me, girlee!" he yelled. Then he hightailed it for the piney woods.

From then on, Callie Ann often saw Mistah Bear lurking at the edge of the woods. Worried, she asked Mose, "What should I do?"

"I got t' go away for a coupla days," Mose said. "Anytime you leave the farm, set out a bowl of milk. If your mamma sees it turn red and boil, that means you're in trouble. Then she's gotta loose the dogs right away."

Shortly after Mose left, two ladies came to the porch where Callie Ann's ma was churning butter. Callie Ann was tying up bean vines nearby. The ladies had pretty fluffed-out petticoats, bonnets with long veils, parasols of green silk, and long white gloves.

"Ma'am," one lady called, "it's so hot, could you please give my sister and me a little honey?"

"Wouldn't you rather have cool water?" asked Callie Ann's mother.

"No, ma'am," said the other lady. "Honey'll perk us up just fine."

So Callie Ann's ma brought out the honey jar and a spoon. Ignoring the spoon, first one lady, then the other ate noisily. Callie Ann whispered, "Mamma! They're lickin' the honey right outta the jar."

"That must be how quality folks eat," her mother said. "Just look how fine they're dressed."

When she gave back the empty jar, the first lady said, "That girlee o' yours looks a clever chile. Could she show us the path through the woods?"

Callie Ann cried, "I don't want t' go!"

But her ma scolded, "Shame on you, carryin' on in front o' quality folks!
Mind your manners and help these nice ladies!"

"Yes'm," Callie Ann said. Before she left, she put out a dish of milk the
way Mose had told her. She said, "Mamma, if this turns red and boils, you
loose the dogs."

When her mother agreed, Callie Ann set off skipping, and the ladies
had to hurry to keep up. Soon they were panting so in their heavy dresses
that they puffed their veils up. Callie Ann spied shaggy brown ears on one
and a furry snout on the other.

She ran for the tallest pine. The ladies dropped to all fours and raced after her. But Callie Ann scrambled up the tree just ahead of them. The first lady called, "Girlee! Come down and show us the path through the woods!"

"Just keep on the way you're going," Callie Ann yelled back.

The second lady shouted, "We'll tell your mamma how bad you are!"

"Just tell her how scared I am o' ladies with fuzzy ears and noses, who run four-legged like critters," Callie Ann answered.

At this the ladies pulled off their dresses and gloves, and Callie Ann saw two big she-bears snarling up at her. They couldn't climb the tree, because they had trimmed their claws to pull on their gloves and shoes.

"Come down here, girlee!" they roared. "We got t' take you t' our brother, Mistah Bear. He's mighty cross with you."

They shook the tree something fierce, and Callie Ann clung for dear life.

Back home the milk in the dish turned red and boiled. So Callie Ann's mamma freed the hounds, who raced for the woods.

When Callie Ann saw them, she yelled, "Here, dogs! Here!"

"Dogs comin'!" warned the first bear.

"Sister, get goin'!" cried the other. Off they bolted, chased by the barking hounds.

Then Callie Ann climbed down. She began walking home, but she was so busy thinking about the bears, she took a wrong turn. At dusk-dark she realized she was lost in the woods.

She was pretty worried until she saw a lighted cabin window.

When no one answered her knock, she pushed open the door.

The place was lit by a chimney fire and candles. A tall mirror on wooden legs stood in one corner. Ashcakes were cooling on the table. Looking out the window behind them, Callie Ann saw a fast-flowing river far below.

Suddenly, through the open door, she spotted Mistah Bear galumphing up the path. He carried a chunk of honeycomb, and angrily rubbed his swollen, bee-stung nose.

Callie Ann slammed and barred the front door.

Mistah Bear rattled it. "Who's in my house?" he demanded.

Callie Ann did not answer.

Mistah Bear pounded on the door. "I brung honey for my ashcakes, and I want 'em 'fore they get cold!"

Callie Ann thought, If Mistah Bear and his sisters can pretend t' be quality folks, I'll pretend t' be a bear.

She dragged a stool over to the door and stood on it.

When Mistah Bear asked again, "Who's there?" Callie Ann cupped her hands and called out in a growly voice, "Bigger Bear."

"I'm the biggest bear around," Mistah Bear roared.

"I'm bigger," the girl yelled back, standing on tiptoe so her mouth was higher than Mistah Bear's head. "Go away, so's I can finish these ashcakes."

"That's my supper!" cried Mistah Bear. He shook the door even harder than before.

"Git! 'fore I have t' come out 'n' whip you!" Callie Ann said. "I already run off two she-bears for practice."

"Them's my sisters!" Mistah Bear cried. "Now I'm boilin' mad!" He threw himself against the door.

Callie Ann poured water on the fire to fill the place with smoke, pinched out all but one candle, then pushed the mirror in front of the window above the river. She put the last lit candle by the mirror, then she hid.

A moment later Mistah Bear broke down the door.

"I'll show you the bigger bear!" he bellowed. Through eye-stinging smoke, Mistah Bear saw his blurry reflection in the candlelit mirror. Thinking it was his rival, he charged. With a crash, Mistah Bear and the mirror tumbled out the window and into the river below, which swept them away.

In the morning Callie Ann found her way home. Her mother hugged her tight, while her dogs jumped up and licked her face. When Mose got back, he laughed loudly to hear how Callie Ann had tricked Mistah Bear.

Before long Callie Ann had Mose for a stepdaddy. Seems her mamma had had enough of folks who only seemed like quality, so she married the real thing. Later Callie Ann had a new sister and brother too.

The farm prospered, and so did the family. And they never had any more trouble with bears neither.

Author's Note

This story is composited and rewritten from two main sources: "Compair Taureau and Jean Malin" in Alcee Fortier's *Louisiana Folk-Tales (Memoirs of the American Folk-Lore Society, Volume II:* 1895) and "The Little Boy and His Dogs" in Joel Chandler Harris's *Daddy Jake, The Runaway and Other Stories by Uncle Remus* (The Century Company, New York: 1889). The instance of Mistah Bear's visit to the farm is loosely based on Fortier; the incident of the disguised "ladies" and the visit to Mistah Bear's cottage are based—again rather loosely—on Harris's narrative.

These tales are grouped by folklorists under the general heading "Escape Up the Tree." It is a familiar story pattern in Africa, the Caribbean, and the American South. A popular variant, "Wiley and the Hairy Man," was collected by Works Progress Administration writers in the South in the 1930's. Elsie Clews Parsons, in her *Folk-Lore of the Antilles, French and English (Memoirs of the American Folk-Lore Society, Volume XXVI, Part III:* 1943), details fourteen Caribbean variants and cites some fifty other versions from Africa to South America.